A GRANDMOTHER'S STORY

A GRANDMOTHER'S STORY

by Glenn Halak

GREEN TIGER PRESS

Published by Simon & Schuster · New York

London · Toronto · Sydney · Tokyo · Singapore

GREEN TIGER PRESS
Simon & Schuster Building
Rockefeller Center
1230 Avenue of the Americas
New York, New York 10020

Designed by Kathleen Westray & Alan Benjamin
Manufactured in the United States of America

10   9   8   7   6   5   4   3   2   1

Library of Congress Cataloging-in-Publication Data
Halak, Glenn.
A grandmother's story / by Glenn Halak.
p.   cm.
Summary: An old woman performs a percipient
rescue of her fisherman grandson after a storm.
[1. Grandmothers—Fiction.   2. Rescue work—
Fiction.   3. Stories in rhyme.]   I. Title.
PZ8.3.H13Gr   1992
[E]—dc20   91-18058   CIP   AC

ISBN 0-671-74953-6

For my grandmother

A GRANDMOTHER'S STORY

There was an old woman who rowed out to sea.

Her neighbors all thought she was mad as could be.

She rowed in the dazzle of dawn's spangled light.

She rowed in the velvety star-studded night.

She rowed when the water was smooth and so still.

She rowed when the waves seemed to travel uphill.

She ate sour apples and drank ginger tea.

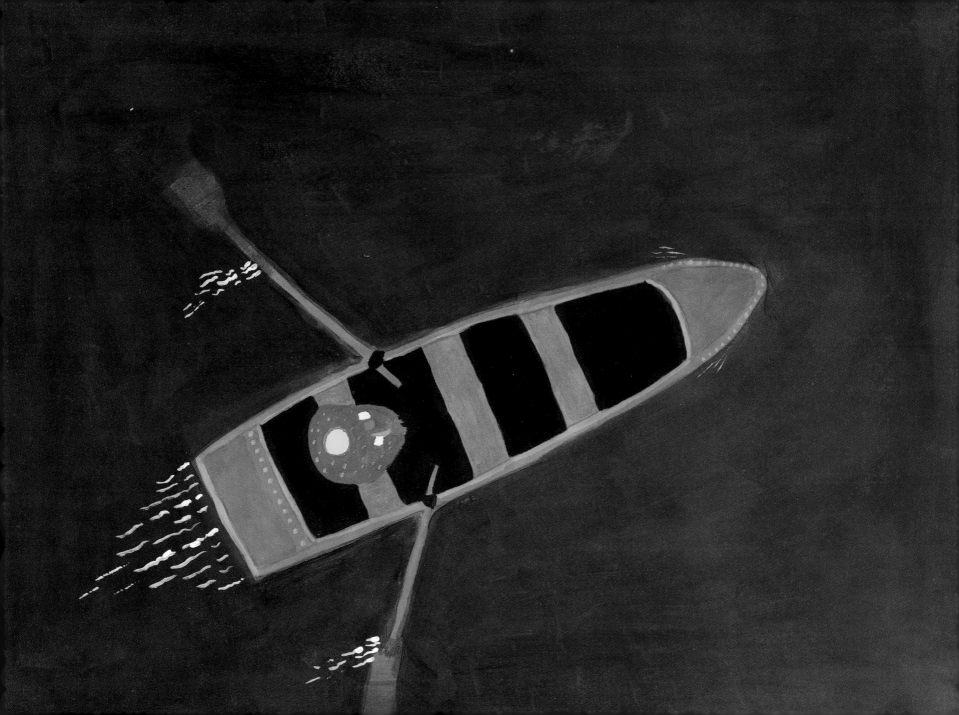

And then she arrived where she knew she must be.

And there she did wait on a cold granite stone,

despite harpoons of lightning and thunder's low moan.

Then after the storm came a dark log a-bobbing,
with a fisherman holding on tightly, and sobbing.

The old lady leaned down and stretched out her hand.
It was her own grandson that she helped to land.

"A miracle, Grandma!" His grateful eyes glistened.
"My dear one," she said, "my heart spoke and I listened."

Then homeward they rowed through the dark and the dew,

all the neighbors amazed when they came into view.

Late that night, with her grandson tucked safely in bed,
all the stars above shining, the old woman said:
"What a wonder the heart is; how wise it can be,
and as strong and as deep as our mother, the sea."

The text of this book is set in 20 pt. Goudy Sans Medium and the display typefaces are Bernhard Antiqua Bold Condensed and Goudy Sans Bold. The illustrations are rendered in watercolor.